Phonics Reading Program

Here Comes Diego!

• The Rain Forest Race • Ice Is Nice • Let's Go See Holes!
• The Great Dinosaur Rescue • Shadow Show • Chinta the Chinchilla

SCHOLASTIC INC.

New York   Toronto   London   Auckland   Sydney
Mexico City   New Delhi   Hong Kong   Buenos Aires

Designed by Kim Brown

Go, Diego, Go!™: The Rain Forest Race (0-439-91311-X) © 2007 Viacom International Inc.
Go, Diego, Go!™: Ice Is Nice (0-439-91312-8) © 2007 Viacom International Inc.
Go, Diego, Go!™: Let's Go See Holes! (0-439-91313-6) © 2007 Viacom International Inc.
Go, Diego, Go!™: The Great Dinosaur Rescue (0-439-91314-4) © 2007 Viacom International Inc.
Go, Diego, Go!™: Shadow Show (0-439-91315-2) © 2007 Viacom International Inc.
Go, Diego, Go!™: Chinta the Chinchilla (0-439-91316-0) © 2007 Viacom International Inc.

ISBN-13: 978-0-439-93228-8
ISBN-10: 0-439-93228-9

12 11 10 9 8 7 6 5 4 3 2   7 8 9 10 11/0

Printed in the U.S.A.
This compilation edition first printing, February 2007

Welcome to the **Go, Diego, Go!** Phonics Reading Program!

Learning to read is so important for your child's success in school and in life. Now **Diego** is here to help your child learn important phonics skills.

Phonics is the fundamental skill of knowing that the letters we read represent the sounds we hear and say. **Diego** helps your child LEARN to read and LOVE to read!

Here's how these readers work:

- At first you may want to read the story to your child.

- Then read together by taking turns line by line or page by page.

- Encourage your child to read the story independently.

- Look for all the words that have the sound being featured in the reader. Read them over and over again.

Scholastic has been encouraging young readers for more than 80 years. Thank you for letting us help you support your beginning reader.

Happy reading,

Francie Alexander
Chief Academic Officer, Scholastic Inc.

In this story, you can learn all about the long "a" sound. Here are some words to sound out.

race   shake   make   gate   pace   place

These are words that you will see in this story and many other stories. You will want to learn them as well.

goes   under   down   slow   fast

These are some more challenging words that you will see in this story.

armadillo	**cannot**	**muddy**
diggers	**might**	**finish**

GO NICK JR DIEGO GO!™

onics Reading Program

Book 1
long a

The Rain Forest Race

by Quinlan B. Lee

We are on Armadillo's **race** team.
Let's get to the start **gate**.
Ready, set, **race**!

The **race** goes under the nut trees.
When the ground **quakes**, it **makes** the trees **shake**.
When the trees **shake**, the nuts fall.

When the trees **shake**, the nuts **make** the other teams slow down.
They cannot keep up their fast **pace**.
What can we do?

Yeah! Armadillo has
a hard shell.
Will you **make** a shell, too?
Lift up your arms and
make a shell!
We **made** it!

It is very muddy in
this **place**.
How can we **make** it
through the mud?
Armadillos are great
diggers!
She can **make** a path.

The other teams are fast!
They might **make** it
to the finish **gate** first.
How can we win the **race**?
What **shape** can Armadillo
make?

She can **make** a ball **shape**
and roll to the finish **gate**.
Curl up and **make** a ball.
Roll, roll, roll!

We **made** it! We won
the **race!**

In this story, you can learn all about the long "i" sound. Here are some words to sound out.

ice   **like**   **slide**   **dive**   **ride**   **bike**

These are words that you will see in this story and many other stories. You will want to learn them as well.

all   **who**   **do**   **down**   **on**

These are some more challenging words that you will see in this story.

Antarctica   **penguin**   **whale**
family   **tummy**   **helped**

Book 2
long i

GO NICK JR.
DIEGO GO!

Phonics Reading Program

Ice Is Nice
by Quinlan B. Lee

Look at all the snow
and **ice**.
I am in Antarctica.
I am here to see penguins.

Penguins **like** snow and **ice**.
They **like** to **slide** on the **ice**.
They **like** to **dive** and swim.

Oh, no!
Baby Penguin did not
dive in.
He is too little to swim.
He is stuck out on the **ice**.
Who can help us?

The blue whale can help.
Blue whales **like** to swim.
I can **slide** on and **ride** to
Baby Penguin.

Now we must get
to Baby Penguin's family.
How can we cross the **ice**?

Baby Penguin can **slide** down the **ice** on his tummy. What do I need to **slide** down the **ice**? A **bike**? A **glider**?

I need a sled to **slide** down the **ice**.
Slide, slide, slide!

We crossed the **ice** and helped Baby Penguin!

In this story, you can learn all about the long "o" sound. Here are some words to sound out.

hole   **poke**   **home**   **scope**   **nose**   **close**

These are words that you will see in this story and many other stories. You will want to learn them as well.

it   **is**   **out**   **see**   **so**

These are some more challenging words that you will see in this story.

something   **until**   **river**
turtle   **asleep**   **spider**

NICK JR.
GO DIEGO GO!™

Phonics Reading Program

Book 3
long o

Let's Go See Holes!

by Quinlan B. Lee

Let's **go** see **holes**!
Hold on and let's **go**!
Do you see any **holes**?
Use your **scope**.

Look, a **hole**!
Did you see something
poke out of the **hole**?
It is a big **nose**.

It is a paca!
He has a big **nose**.
He is asleep.
He does not **go** out
until the sun sets.

Use your **scope**
and look **close** to the river.
It is a **hole**.
Is this **hole** a **home**?
Let's **go** see!

Why is this **hole so close** to the river?
Let's read the **note**.
It is a river turtle nest.

Let's find one more **hole**.
Did you see something
poke out?
What do you think it is?
Is it a **mole**?

No! It is a spider.
This **hole** is his **home**.
He was asleep.
When the sun went down,
he **woke** up.

It is great to discover **holes**!
Now it is time to **go home**.

In this story, you can learn all about the long "u" sound. Here are some words to sound out.

huge   **clue**   **use**   **dune**

These are words that you will see in this story and many other stories. You will want to learn them as well.

the   **help**   **your**   **their**   **tail**

These are some more challenging words that you will see in this story.

dinosaur	**family**	**climb**
watch	**rescue**	**good-bye**

The Great Dinosaur Rescue

by Quinlan B. Lee

The dinosaur is **huge**.
She could **use** our help.
She wants to find her family.

Where did her family go?
Do you see a **clue**?
There are prints in
the **dune**.

Those prints were
a good **clue**.
Now **use** the scope to
find her family.
We have to climb over
these **dunes** and go up
that **huge** slope.

Let's go over the **dunes** and up the slope.
Watch out!
It is a rock slide.
What can we **use** that is soft to land on?
Rescue Pack can help us!

Thanks, **Rescue** Pack!
Now let's **use** the dinosaur's
huge tail to climb back up to
her family.

Use your hands and
let's go!
Let's go up the **huge** tail.
We did it!

It is the dinosaur's family.
They are so big.
Look at their **huge** smiles
for their baby.

Good-bye, dinosaur.
We love to **rescue**!

In this story, you can learn all about the "sh" sound. Here are some words to sound out.

shadow   show   shiny   shapes   sheds   shell

These are words that you will see in this story and many other stories. You will want to learn them as well.

its   this   have   what   great

These are some more challenging words that you will see in this story.

animal	**better**	**armadillo**
slowly	**upside**	**sloth**

GO NICK JR.
DiEGO GO!™

Phonics Reading Program

Book 5
sh

Shadow Show

by Quinlan B. Lee

Let's play **shadow shapes**.
I'll **show** you how.
This animal **sheds** its skin.
What is it?

It is a snake.
It **sheds** its skin when
it grows.
Then it grows **shiny**
new skin.

What animal **shape** is this?
It has a hard **shell**.
It can dig better than a
shovel.

It is an armadillo.
Its **shell** protects its
soft body.
It digs with its **sharp** claws.

Whose **shadow** is this?
This animal moves slowly.
It likes to hang upside down.

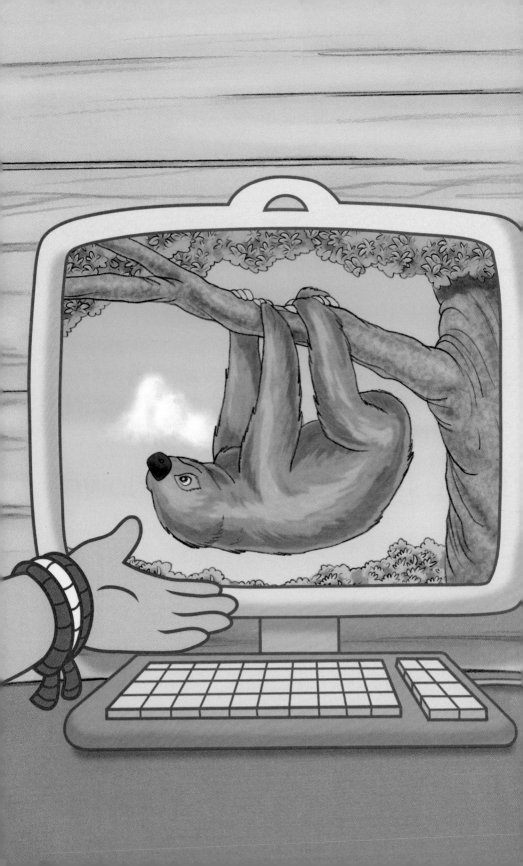

It is a sloth.
Sloths are **shy**.
They have **sharp** claws.

What animal **shape** is this?
You ride in a **ship** to see
this animal.
It is a **fish** with **sharp** teeth.

It is a **shark**.
Great work!

In this story, you can learn all about the "ch" sound. Here are some words to sound out.

Chinta   change   reach   choose   chomp   chinchilla

These are words that you will see in this story and many other stories. You will want to learn them as well.

our   over   into   now   have

These are some more challenging words that you will see in this story.

waterfall   hungry   mountain
rocky   happy   glider

NICK JR

GO DIEGO GO!

Phonics Reading Program

Book 6
ch

Chinta the Chinchilla

by Quinlan B. Lee

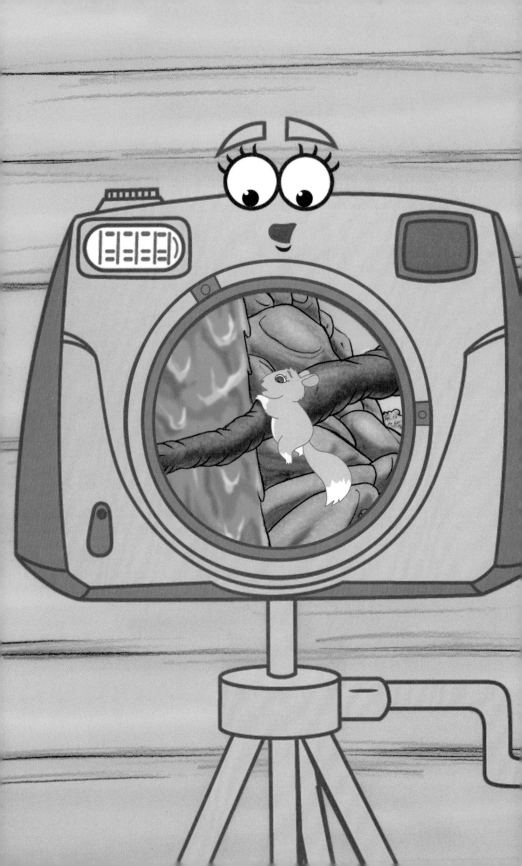

Chinta the **Chinchilla** needs our help.
She is on a **branch** over a waterfall.
We need to **catch** her!

Rescue Pack can **change** to help us.
Will he **change** into a bike or a hang glider?
You **choose**!

Now **reach** out and **catch**
Chinta the **Chinchilla**.
Reach, reach, reach!
We got her!

Chinta the **Chinchilla**
is hungry.
Chinchillas eat plants.
Watch her **chomp**!

Let's take **Chinta** the **Chinchilla** home. **Chinchillas** live in the mountains. **Check** the scope for **Chinchilla** Mountain.

It is **chilly**.
Chinchillas have fur
to keep them warm.
I can keep warm
if I **change** my clothes.

Chinchilla Mountain is very rocky.
Chinchillas hop up the mountain.
Hop, hop, hop!

Chinta the **Chinchilla** is happy to be back on **Chinchilla** Mountain. Great work!